FERN VALLEY

A Collection of Short Stories

written by
Aileen Stewart

Tate Publishing *& Enterprises*

Published by Tate Publishing & Enterprises, LLC
127 E. Trade Center Terrace | Mustang, Oklahoma 73064 USA
1.888.361.9473 | www.tatepublishing.com

Tate Publishing is committed to excellence in the publishing industry. The company reflects the philosophy established by the founders, based on Psalm 68:11,
"The Lord gave the word and great was the company of those who published it."

Book design copyright © 2010 by Tate Publishing, LLC. All rights reserved.
Cover and interior design by Chris Webb
Illustrations by Greg White

Published in the United States of America

ISBN: 978-1-61739-527-7
1. Juvenile Fiction / Animals / Farm Animals
2. Juvenile Fiction / Social Issues / Values & Virtues
10.12.21

Dedication

To Bobby and Emily, my two biggest fans.

Table of Contents

The Club

Roberta and Mildred Cornstalk lived on a little farm outside of Fern Valley with their mama and papa and their little brother, Edward. They were two ordinary-looking chickens, but they had very good imaginations.

Early one morning, Roberta and Mildred were sitting under the big apple tree in the front yard trying to think of something that would cheer them up. They were both sad because their Granny Cornstalk had gone to be with Grandpa Cornstalk in heaven.

"What if we formed a club?" said Roberta.

"What kind of a club and who will be members?"

"Well," said Roberta, "maybe we could have an afternoon tea club."

"Oh, what fun! We could dress up and invite Kimmy Curlytail and Betsy Woolrich."

Kimmy was a cute little pig that lived on the farm next door with her mama and papa and six brothers. Betsy was a sweet lamb who was staying with Grandma and Grandpa Woolrich and her uncle, John. Betsy's parents were touring the United States looking for customers to buy their hand-knitted sweaters.

Roberta and Mildred thought it would be nice to have their afternoon tea club meet every Wednesday in the old garden shed behind their house. Mama Cornstalk gave them some paper and envelopes to make invitations. When they finished, they asked her if they could deliver the invitations in person. Mama agreed, and two very excited, giggling girls set out on their delivery journey.

As they neared the Curlytail farm, they saw Kimmy swinging on a tire swing that Pa Curlytail had attached to a strong branch of an apple tree. She saw them coming, stopped swinging, and ran to meet them. "What are you all up to?"

"We came to invite you to our new tea club," they said together.

"Cool, when is it?"

"It's going to be this Wednesday at noon," said Mildred as she jumped up and down excitedly.

Roberta and Mildred spent a few more minutes talking with Kimmy, and then they headed to Betsy's house. Betsy only lived five minutes from Kimmy, so the girls were there in no time at all. They went up the front steps and rang the doorbell. Betsy's uncle answered the door.

"Is Betsy here?" asked Roberta.

"No, she and her grandma ran into town to do some errands."

The girls looked at each other in disappointment and then back at John. Holding out the invitation, Roberta asked if he would make sure Betsy received it.

"Of course, girls. I will put it in my shirt pocket so I don't forget."

Roberta and Mildred thanked him and headed back home. Roberta had a crush on John, so Mildred just smiled when she said, "He is terribly nice."

"Yes," said Mildred, "I think you are right. Now let's plan what we shall wear."

The sisters rummaged through the old trunk that Granny had given them. The old trunk was large and black and contained an array of bonnets, floppy sun hats, beads, aprons, scarves, and brooches. Although

Roberta was one year older than Mildred, she let her choose first.

"Oh," said Mildred, "it's really hard to decide because everything is so lovely." She finally decided on a big, red, floppy sun hat; a red and white checkered apron with a white lace ruffle; and some nice red beads.

Roberta looked everything over very carefully before making her final selection. She chose a blue hat with a wide brim and an equally wide white ribbon. She also chose a nice yellow scarf, which she put around her neck, pinning it together with a small daisy-shaped brooch.

Now all that was left to do was to plan the menu and clean and decorate the garden shed. They decided to clean the shed first. Mama gave them some old rags and a pail of water to clean the windows, but before they could clean the windows, they had to move Mama's extra flowerpots into the corner.

Soon the girls had everything looking tidy. All the pots were stacked in the far left-hand corner of the shed in groups of three. The windows sparkled brightly in the afternoon sun, and the floor had been swept clean of dirt and old leaves.

In the shed, they also found an old card table and four chairs, which Mama said they could use. In addition, she gave them an old white bed sheet to use as a tablecloth. A mason jar filled with flowers completed the table. As they stood back to admire all their hard work, Roberta took Mildred by the wing.

"Isn't it marvelous?" she whispered. "It will be just like having tea at the Glitz."

The Glitz was a small but extremely fashionable restaurant in town where everyone always wore their Sunday clothes. Granny Cornstalk had taken the girls there once before their little brother, Edward, was born.

The girls had worked so hard that before they knew it, it was time for supper, a bath, and bed. Mama tucked each girl in and kissed them soundly. "Papa will be in to kiss you goodnight in just a moment," she said as she left the room. While the girls waited for Papa to finish tucking Edward into his bed, Roberta told Mildred that they would decide upon a menu the next day.

"Yes," said Mildred, "and maybe Mama will let us use the fancy teacups and little matching plates."

"Perhaps if we are very, very careful."

Just then, Papa strode in, kissed the girls goodnight, and turned out the light. Each girl snuggled into her bed, and soon they were both fast asleep dreaming of a special garden shed and the good times they were going to have with their friends.

The next morning arrived bright and beautiful with the sun streaming cheerfully through the pink ruffled curtains that hung jauntily in the two bedroom windows. Roberta awoke, opening first one eye and then the other. When she realized it was morning, she threw back her pink and green patchwork quilt and quickly jumped out of bed.

"Mildred, are you awake?" she asked as she shook her sister ever so gently.

Mildred yawned and said, "Yes, Roberta," even though her eyes were still tightly closed. Mildred liked to take her time getting up each morning, while Roberta liked to get up fast and get the day started. They might have been sisters and best friends, but they were definitely as different as night and day.

"Today we can plan our menu," Roberta said. This comment caught Mildred's attention, and she finally opened her eyes.

"All right, but let's have breakfast first," she said as a loud rumble came from the general direction of her stomach. Both girls laughed as Mildred threw back her matching quilt and crawled out of bed. They hurried downstairs to breakfast only to find Edward already at the table eating Mama's famous poppy seed muffins and drinking a large glass of ice-cold milk.

Mama's poppy seed muffins were famous all over Fern Valley. She had even won a blue ribbon for them at the county fair two years in a row. The girls looked at each other and said at the exact same time, "We should have muffins with our tea." Mama, who was standing by the oven holding a fresh batch, just smiled. Soon the girls were sitting beside Edward munching on their own muffins and drinking milk. Between bites, they decided on cucumber sandwiches with the crusts removed, mint tea, and poppy seed muffins with homemade strawberry jam. Edward just rolled his eyes.

After breakfast, the girls washed the morning dishes, made their beds, brushed their teeth, and headed for the garden to pick the mint leaves and fresh cucumbers they needed for Wednesday.

"Do you know what?" said Mildred.

"No," said Roberta, "but I'm sure you are going to tell me."

"I've been thinking that it might be nice to fold table napkins into little fans for tomorrow."

The summer before, the girls had seen a napkin folding demonstration at the library. Henrietta Redfeather, Fern Valley's assistant librarian and the most attractive single turkey in three counties, had shown everyone who attended her class how to fold napkins in six different styles. Mildred remembered exactly how to fold the fan style because it was the easiest.

"Well," said Mildred, "what do you think?" She looked intently at Roberta while Roberta thought about the idea. Roberta always liked to think things through before answering.

"That would be wonderful," she replied, "but what will we use for napkin rings?"

"I hadn't thought about that," said Mildred. The two girls thought and thought for what seemed like a really long time. "I've got it," said Mildred, vigorously shaking the fat cucumber she was still holding. "We can make napkin rings out of the empty paper towel tube that I saw in the kitchen this morning. We can cut it into pieces, and then we can glue fabric scraps around each piece."

Roberta thought that to be a fine idea, so both girls hurried to finish picking the mint and cucumbers and ran back to the house with their little garden baskets bumping at their sides.

"Oh good," said Mildred as she spied the paper towel tube still lying on the counter, "Mama didn't throw it away yet."

The girls spent the rest of the afternoon making napkin rings. Mama had given them enough fabric scraps to make two yellow rings and two green rings. They then folded four white cloth napkins into fans and used the rings to keep each fan from unfolding. That night the girls could barely sleep due to the excitement that tomorrow was sure to bring.

When Wednesday morning finally arrived, the girls awoke with feelings of great anticipation. They raced each other downstairs and found they had beaten Edward to the breakfast table. They quickly ate their cornflakes, brushed their teeth, and got dressed so they could start making cucumber sandwiches. They didn't need to make the tea until right before Kimmy and Betsy would arrive, and there was already a tray of muffins left over from the day before.

"Roberta, get a jar of strawberry jam from the pantry," said Mama. "And I will get the teacups and plates from the sideboard."

It seemed like it was taking noontime forever to arrive, but eventually it was ten till the hour. The girls began taking things out to the shed, and Mama put the water on to boil for the tea. At exactly twelve o'clock, they saw Betsy walking up the front lane.

"Betsy's here," they cried in unison and ran to meet her.

"Oh, Betsy," Mildred said. "You are the first one to arrive, and we're so glad you could come!" Then the girls noticed that Kimmy was also coming up the lane. The four girls chattered excitedly.

Mama said, "Why don't you girls all go out to the shed, and I will bring the tea out to you in just a few minutes." So off they went.

Roberta and Mildred had butterflies in their stomachs. What would Kimmy and Betsy think about the shed and the tea club? But they needn't have worried, because as soon as they opened the shed door both guests were *ooh-ing* and *ahh-ing*.

"What a beautiful table," said Betsy.

"Oh, yes," said Kimmy, "and look at the lovely sandwiches and muffins." Moments later, Mama Cornstalk arrived with the tea.

Roberta picked up the delicate teapot and in her best Mama voice asked Betsy, "Would you like some tea, madam?" This started all the girls to giggling. She was laughing so hard she almost spilled the tea she was trying to pour in Betsy's cup. Once she was calm, she poured everyone some tea and passed around the plate of sandwiches.

"I would give this restaurant four stars," said Kimmy in a high voice. She was trying to sound like a movie star she had once seen on television, but it came out sounding more like a squeaky teenage boy whose voice was changing. This caused the girls to start laughing again. The girls were having so much fun imitating adults and having snacks that two hours had passed before they knew it. Reluctantly, Betsy and Kimmy got ready to go home.

"This was so much fun," said Kimmy.

"Yes, it was, and I can't wait till next Wednesday," Betsy added.

Roberta and Mildred waved good-bye to their friends until they could no longer see them on the road. They then went back in the shed and began to clean up. As they finished cleaning, they thought about how nice their first tea had been. "I hope Granny won't mind that we weren't sad today," said Mildred.

Roberta thought a moment and then replied, "I don't think she minded, Mildred. And just maybe Granny had her own tea club today with Grandpa and all their new friends in heaven."

"Maybe," said Mildred, smiling. And with that thought, the two girls finished cleaning up the remnants of their party.

The Brothers

Although Edward Cornstalk often thought his sisters, Roberta and Mildred, were really weird, his opinion of them went up when they allowed him to tag along on trips to Kimmy Curlytail's house. This was because Kimmy, the cute little pig who lived next door, had six brothers. There was Johnny, who could climb the biggest trees around. There was

Jimmy, who always had a funny story to tell. There was Jaimie, who could throw a great fastball and an even better curveball. There was Jared, who was quiet and liked to read books. There was Jason, who liked to build things. And there was Justin, who liked to collect things. With six different brothers to play with, Edward was always bound to have a good time. He was especially glad to be going with his sisters today because he was tired of playing by himself.

"Wash up before you go," said Mama Cornstalk.

Edward wondered what difference it would make since the dirt he had been playing in was the same color as his feathers.

As Edward washed his face and wings, he heard his sister Mildred hollering up the stairs, "Hurry up, Edward; Roberta and I are ready to go."

"I'm coming," Edward hollered back. He quickly finished washing and ran down the stairs. He certainly didn't want to be left behind!

As the three young chickens set out, Edward thought about the last time he had been to the Curlytails' house. They had a nice, big, red barn where Pa Curlytail kept his tractor and other farm equipment. Since Pa had been out plowing the corn and bean fields, Edward and the other boys had played in the barn. They had climbed the wooden ladder that went up to the loft and had swung on the giant rope that hung from the ceiling. As a big finale, each boy had dropped into the large pile of hay being stored in the loft. Edward wondered if today was going to be a rope swinging day.

It only took five minutes to get to the Curlytail farm, where Kimmy was waiting at the front gate. "Hi, Roberta. Hi, Mildred," said Kimmy. "Hi, Edward, Justin is on the front porch."

Edward found Justin sitting on the front porch surrounded by piles of rubber bands. There was a pile of small red and green bands like the kind that come on a weekday newspaper, there was a pile of fat beige bands like the kind that come on a thick Sunday newspaper, and there was a pile of really small yellow bands like the kind Mama Cornstalk used in the garden when she wanted to keep the parsley in bunches.

"Whatcha doin'?" asked Edward.

"I'm sorting my rubber band collection," Justin replied. "Then I'm going to put each different kind of band in a separate jar. That way, when I need a certain kind it will be easy to find."

"Oh," said Edward, sitting down beside him. "Where are the other boys?"

"Johnny and Jaimie are helping Pa repair the fence at the back of the property, and Jared is in town at the library. I'm not sure where Jimmy and Jason are."

Edward picked up one of the fat beige bands and looked around. Kimmy, Roberta, and Mildred were still standing at the gate chattering away like girls often do. Without thinking, Edward took aim and let the band fly. Unfortunately for Roberta, Edward's aim was very good.

"Ouch!" she yelled and then began to rub her tail feathers. "Edward! You are going to be in big trouble when I catch you."

Ma Curlytail came to the front door to see what the commotion was all about. When she finally understood what had occurred, she told the two boys to find something more constructive to do.

"I'm sorry I got you into trouble, Justin," Edward said sincerely. "I didn't think I was going to hit anyone."

"That's all right. I'll put these bands away, and then we can go fishing at the pond."

The pond was in a meadow surrounded by ferns in the middle of the Big Woods. The Big

Woods were so big, in fact, that they ran beside and behind the Woolrich Ranch, behind both the Cornstalk and Curlytail farms, and all the way to the back edge of town. The Big Woods' pond was a favorite fishing spot for the boys, who frequently caught fat yellow sunfish and occasionally a stray snapping turtle.

Justin put his collection away in his room, and he and Edward headed for the barn to get a couple of fishing poles. On the way to the barn, they met Jimmy, who decided to go with them. The three boys gathered up their poles, stopped back at the house to get some bread for bait, and started on their way to the pond. Along the way they did all the things that little boys do. They found sturdy sticks to walk with, they threw pinecones as far as they possibly could, they whistled a catchy tune, and they investigated some squirrel tracks. By and by they reached the pond.

Once there, the boys circled the pond trying to decide on the best spot to start fishing. They had gone about halfway around when they spied a fallen tree lying partially in the water.

"This tree wasn't here last time," said Jimmy. "It must have fallen during that big storm we had two days ago."

Naturally, the boys had to check out the fallen tree, which was a scraggly old pine. Jimmy set down his pole, jumped onto the tree, and started making his way toward the end submerged in water.

"You had better be careful," said Justin. Justin was always very cautious.

"Yeah, yeah, yeah," said Jimmy, who was inching his way toward the branches. Jimmy was trying to make his way around a particularly gnarled branch when his right leg suddenly slipped off the tree trunk. Edward and Justin saw him wave his arms wildly in the air just before splashing into the edge of the shallow but very muddy pond.

Jimmy stood up and tried to climb back onto the tree, but he was stuck in mud up to his knees.

"Somebody help me outta here!" he shouted.

Edward and Justin looked at each other, and Edward said, "I'll go get him."

After laying his pole beside Jimmy's, he carefully worked his way toward the gnarled limb where Jimmy had slipped. He held on to the limb with his left wing and offered the other to Jimmy.

"Take my wing," he said.

Jimmy did as he was instructed, but the mud had a firm grip on his feet. Edward pulled, but Jimmy barely budged.

"Justin, I think we're going to need your help too," groaned Edward as he gave Jimmy's hand one more hard tug. Before Justin could even reply, there was a second big splash, and two boys were now standing knee deep in mud.

Justin started laughing so hard that tears streamed down his face. "If you guys think

I'm going to climb out there and end up stuck in the mud like you, you're crazy," he said. As he stood there laughing, he was suddenly pummeled in the head with mud balls. "That's not fair," he said while backing out of range. Despite the attack, he still laughed.

Jimmy and Edward wiggled and squirmed and squirmed and wiggled until they were finally able to pull themselves loose from the mud. Finally reaching dry ground again, they joined in with Justin's laughter. They were all ridiculously dirty.

So much for washing up before I came, thought Edward.

The three very muddy little boys picked up their poles and headed back to the Curlytail farm. On the way, the mud began to dry, making the boys all very itchy. When they arrived, they ran into Johnny, who started howling.

"You should see how funny the three of you look," he said.

Just then, Ma Curlytail looked out the back porch door. "Oh my," she said between chuckles. "These can't be the same boys that left here an hour ago, because they were all nice and clean."

The boys hosed off by the barn before going in the house to take a bath in the family's big claw-foot tub. Ma Curlytail washed their clothes while they bathed and then set three glasses of milk and three plates of cookies on the table. Edward put on a pair of clean overalls, borrowed from Justin, while his clothes dried out on the clothesline.

As the boys sat down at the kitchen table to eat their snacks, everyone, including Roberta, Mildred, and Kimmy, gathered around to hear what happened. Edward and Justin let Jimmy tell the story because he told a story better than anyone else they knew. Everyone listened and laughed. Edward smiled to himself and thought about what an interesting day it had turned out to be.

The Surprise

Betsy Woolrich was going to have a birthday on Saturday, and Grandma Woolrich had promised her a party. Betsy eagerly sat down to make out her invitations, six in all. There was an invitation for Roberta and Mildred Cornstalk, who lived down the lane; an invitation for Kimmy Curlytail, who lived next door; an invitation for Sammie Gruff, a friend from school who lived in town; an invitation for Alice Redfeather, another friend from school who lived in town; an invitation for Uncle Bertram and Aunt Beatrice, who lived in Muddy Springs; and an invitation for Cousin Iris, who happened to be Fern Valley's schoolteacher as well as a relative.

Betsy was extremely excited. There was going to be cake and ice cream, balloons and streamers, party hats and games, and friends and family. The only thing that would be missing from her party was the presence of Mama and Papa Woolrich. Mama and Papa Woolrich were traveling across the United States on business. Right now, they were hundreds of miles away at the Crystal Springs Ski Resort taking orders for their hand-knitted sweaters.

Betsy finished her invitations, sealed them up in their envelopes, and put a stamp on each one. As she walked to the mailbox, she wondered if Mama and Papa would call her on her birthday. "That would be nice," she said to a robin eating worms in the front yard. "I've never had a long-distance call before."

Betsy happened to reach the mailbox at the exact same time as Uncle Cyrus, the mailman. Cyrus Gruff, who was called Uncle Cyrus by friends and family alike, was the oldest goat in Fern Valley and had been delivering mail long before Betsy was even born. He had a long white beard, bushy white eyebrows, and a deep, raspy voice.

"Hello, Betsy," Uncle Cyrus said happily.

"Hello, Uncle Cyrus," Betsy replied. "Here are my birthday invitations. I sure hope Sammie will be able to come."

"Oh, I'm sure she will. She might even bring you a nice present," he said with a wink. And with that, he took Betsy's invitations and left to finish the rest of his mail route.

Walking back to the house, Betsy thought about what a long wait it was going to be until her birthday since it was only Tuesday. Betsy was thinking so hard that she ran into her uncle, John, and fell with a thump onto the dusty drive. In one amazing swoop, John picked Betsy up and set her back on her feet.

"Sorry, Uncle John," she said. "I wasn't looking where I was going."

"That's all right, Betsy," he said with a grin. "I bet you had much more important things on your mind." He waved and quickly set off again.

Back at the house, Betsy found Grandma Woolrich sitting on the front porch swing shelling peas. Grandma was singing her favorite hymn, "Amazing Grace." Betsy sat down in a nearby rocker and joined in with Grandma's singing. Their voices blended together so well that even the birds chirping in the old elm tree stopped to listen. When the song ended, they looked at each other and smiled.

"That was really lovely, dear," said Grandma Woolrich. "How about singing 'The Old Rugged Cross'?" The two sat and kept on singing, and before they knew it, Grandma had shelled a whole bushel of sweet green peas. "Well now," said Grandma, "all that singing has made me hungry. Why don't we go in and start fixing lunch?"

For the next two days, Betsy was so busy helping Grandma can the peas, beans, beets, and carrots from their garden that she didn't even think once about her upcoming birthday or party. But when Betsy went to fetch the mail on Friday, she was reminded. There, amongst the bills and junk mail, was a beautiful postcard from Mama and Papa Woolrich. On the front was a picture of two skiers in big fluffy jackets, and on the back it said that Mama and Papa were selling so many sweaters that Betsy could look forward to a big surprise for her birthday. Betsy wondered what in the world the surprise could be.

"Grandma, Grandma," Betsy cried as she ran into the house. Grandma was standing in the large but homey kitchen washing dishes. "Mama and Papa are sending me a surprise for my birthday. Do you know what it is?"

Grandma paused to wipe her hands on a dishtowel and then turned to speak to Betsy. "If I did, do you think I would tell you?"

Betsy laughed. "No, I guess that would ruin the surprise."

To keep Betsy from thinking about the surprise too much, Grandma Woolrich sent her out to pick raspberries for the birthday cake she was baking. She was soon done picking berries, but Grandma had a whole list of other things for her to do that kept her busy the whole rest of the day.

Betsy awoke on Saturday morning with a feeling of great excitement. She quickly made her big double bed, making sure she smoothed out all the wrinkles in the crisply laundered sheets and the sunny yellow comforter. She then ran to pull up the window shades. As she looked outside, she could see that it was a beautiful summer day. Downstairs she could hear Grandma in the kitchen making breakfast. As she walked down the hall, she could smell blueberry pancakes, which were her favorite.

She ran down the stairs and into the kitchen, where she found Grandpa and Uncle John already eating. "Come join us, birthday girl," said Grandpa Woolrich in his deep voice.

"Yes!" said Uncle John. "We might have saved you a pancake or two."

They all laughed as Grandma set a plate of fresh, hot, blueberry pancakes in front of her, and Grandpa passed her the maple syrup.

"Well," said Grandma, "are you ready for your big day?"

"Oh, yes, I can hardly wait for everyone to get here."

After breakfast, Grandma and Betsy began to decorate the living room. They hung pink, crepe-paper streamers and pink and white balloons. Grandma set the beautiful cake decorated with fluffy white frosting and fresh raspberries next to the party hats on a table in the corner. She then went back to the kitchen to make some punch. As Betsy looked around admiringly, she could hear Grandpa and Uncle John filling up a washtub outside for the apple bobbing contest. She smiled to herself and thought what a wonderful day it was going to be.

When it was almost time for the guests to arrive, Betsy went to her room to change into her brand new party dress. It was white with a row of tiny pink roses at the waist. She completed the outfit with a large pink hair bow, which she delicately placed over one ear. While she was finishing up, she heard Uncle Bertram and Aunt Beatrice laughing with Grandpa and Uncle John in the front yard. She hurried down to greet them and the other guests that would soon be arriving.

Roberta, Mildred, and Kimmy arrived together shortly after Betsy's aunt and uncle. "Happy birthday, Betsy!" the three girls shouted. Betsy thanked them and showed them where to put the presents that each one was carrying. Sammie arrived next, carrying a package wrapped in pink polka-dotted paper. About five minutes later, Cousin Iris and Alice peddled up the drive on their bicycles. Each one had a gaily wrapped package in her bicycle basket.

Everyone Betsy had invited had arrived, so Grandma led them all into the living room. Everyone chatted while Grandma served punch. Grandma then put candles on the cake.

"Okay, everyone," she said loudly to be heard over all of the noise. "Let's all sing 'Happy Birthday.'" Everyone began singing, so no one heard the front door open or noticed the two extra guests that joined the back of the group.

"Birthday blessings and wishes for the best day ever," Grandma whispered into Betsy's ear as she lit the candles. Betsy smiled at Grandma Woolrich and blew out the candles ever so gently. When she looked up, there stood Mama and Papa Woolrich. Betsy closed her eyes and opened them again just to be sure she wasn't imagining things.

"Surprise," said Mama.

"Surprise," said Papa.

Betsy immediately ran and hugged them both as tightly as possible. "This is the best surprise ever," she said happily, and she gave each of her parents another big hug.

The Twins

The summer had flown by, and before everyone knew it, it was time to start a new school year. Iris Woolrich, Fern Valley's teacher, had spent a whole week preparing lessons and getting the classroom ready. Several of the town's men had put a fresh coat of red paint on the little schoolhouse, and the women had washed the windows until they sparkled like diamonds. Mr. Bigpaw, who published Fern Valley's weekly paper, the *F.V. Gazette*, even climbed a tall ladder borrowed from the firehouse to polish the school bell.

Mr. Bigpaw was also Tommy and Abigail's daddy. This was going to be Tommy and Abigail's first year at school, and they were really looking forward to the event. Their mommy, Mrs. Bigpaw, had sewn each of the twins a new outfit. She had sewn a little purple dress with matching pantaloons and a big white collar for Abigail, and she had sewn a durable pair of blue overalls with brown corduroy pockets for Tommy.

The first day of school arrived, and Abigail and Tommy tingled with excitement from the tops of their long ears all the way down to their little bunny toes. They quickly ate their breakfast, grabbed the sack lunches Mommy Bigpaw had lovingly prepared, and ran all the way to the schoolhouse. It was still quite early, so they sat on the front steps to wait.

"I wonder when everyone else is going to get here," Tommy said. Just then they saw the seven Curlytail children coming down the lane. Tommy ran off to greet the boys. "Hey, guys," said Tommy proudly.

"Hi," they all replied as they made their way to the playground.

Tommy was thrilled to have a chance to hang out with the older boys. He and Abigail knew everyone from summer Bible school, but the chance to see them almost every day was like a dream come true for the little boy. Abigail, who had remained patiently on the front steps, smiled at Kimmy, who sat down beside her.

"Hello, Abigail," said Kimmy. "Are you excited about starting school today?"

"Oh yes," said Abigail a bit breathlessly. "I have been practicing my ABC's all summer. Would you like to hear them?" Kimmy nodded.

As Kimmy listened to Abigail recite her letters, other children began arriving. Roberta and Mildred Cornstalk came down the lane practically dragging their brother, Edward. Edward didn't like school much. Next, Betsy Woolrich arrived in an old blue pickup truck driven by Uncle John.

Moments later, Sammie Gruff and Alice Redfeather joined Kimmy and Abigail on the front stoop.

"Hi, Kimmy. Hi, Abigail," said Alice cheerfully. "Are you both ready for the first day of school?"

"Yes," said Kimmy. "As a matter of fact, Abigail was just reciting her ABC's for me, and she didn't miss a single letter." Abigail's cheeks turned a rosy shade of red, but she felt really special. After all, it wasn't every day that the older girls paid such attention to her.

Nathan Gruff, Sammie's cousin, was the last to arrive, but he had no sooner joined the other boys on the playground when the school bell rang out loud and clear. Everyone hurried in and found a desk at which to sit. The older children all sat at the desks they had used the year before, leaving the front two desks open for Tommy and Abigail. When everyone was finally seated, Iris Woolrich began, "For those of you who are new, I am your teacher, Miss Iris. Today we will begin with each of you telling the class what you did over the summer."

As the other children told tales of fishing and swimming, clubs and parties, and visiting relatives, Abigail looked interestedly around the room. Behind Miss Iris's desk was a large blackboard and a tray that held white chalk and erasers. On the desk sat a pencil can filled with bright yellow pencils and a box of tissues. To the right of the blackboard and desk hung a world map and to the left a clock. Abigail was so busy looking at all the things in the room that she didn't realize Miss Iris was speaking to her.

Everyone in the classroom began snickering, causing Abigail to look up. Miss Iris just smiled and winked at her. "And what did you do this summer?" she asked Abigail once more.

"Well," said Abigail shyly, "I practiced my ABC's all summer long, and I can even draw them on paper now."

"Very good," said Miss Iris. "Maybe before the day is over you can show the class what you know. Now how about you, Tommy? What did you do this summer?"

Tommy smiled broadly and began to tell how he had gone to the big city with his dad. "Dad had to interview some important guy at the 'lectric company. That was kind of boring, but when they were done he took me to a fancy restaurant, and I had a huge piece of chocolate cake."

When the school day finally came to an end and all the children were dismissed, the twins headed for home. Abigail was so overcome with the excitement of the day that she held Tommy's hand all the way home. Tommy was so overwhelmed himself that he let Abigail hold his hand and never once tried to pull away. Mommy Bigpaw met them at the door, and she knew from the expressions on their faces that their first day at school had been a big success.

As the days went by, the children began to develop a routine. Most of them came to school ten or fifteen minutes early to play on the playground. Then, after the school bell had rung, it was time for lessons in writing, reading, and spelling, followed by lunch and recess. After recess, there were lessons in math and geography, and finally, it was time to go home.

August and September passed pleasantly this way, but October held a surprise for everyone. It seemed like an ordinary Monday to the children, who were sitting quietly at their desks waiting for Miss Iris to collect their homework. But instead of collecting their work, Miss Iris had an announcement.

"Children," she said in her firm but sweet voice, "today we are going to break from our routine so we can start a class project." She kept speaking as she passed out small slips of paper to each child. "We are going to put on a play for all the parents and townsfolk two weeks from now. The papers I have just given you describe the part each of you will be playing."

As everyone looked at their slip of paper excitedly, they discovered that the play was going to be about nutrition. Kimmy was going to represent the dairy group as a piece of cheese. Her brothers were each going to be a different kind of fruit. Edward was to be a peanut butter sandwich, and his sisters were to be cereal and toast. Betsy was going to be a bottle of water and Sammy a glass of milk. Alice, Nathan, and the twins were all going to be vegetables. Alice would be an ear of corn,

Nathan a pea pod, and Tommy and Abigail were both to be carrots.

Miss Iris told everyone that since the school was too small to hold all the guests, the play was going to be held at the town hall next to the fire station. She also stated that Mr. Bigpaw had volunteered to announce the play in the newspaper's "Upcoming Events" section, and Mrs. Bigpaw and Nathan's mother, Silvia Gruff, had volunteered to sew costumes. Sixteen very excited children left school that day, but none were more excited than Tommy and Abigail.

Tommy and Abigail thought that it was super neat that they were going to be twin carrots, and they could talk of nothing else all the way home. They were still eagerly discussing their role as carrots when Mommy Bigpaw set a carrot casserole on the dinner table. They looked at each other and burst out laughing.

"What's so funny?" asked Mrs. Bigpaw, and that made the twins laugh even harder.

During the next two weeks, all the children worked very hard memorizing their lines, while Mrs. Bigpaw and Mrs. Gruff frantically sewed costumes. Finally, the night of the play arrived. All the children put on their costumes and stood on the stage behind a big curtain. They could hear all the adults whispering softly on the other side and this made Abigail very nervous. Tommy sensed it and gave her paw a little squeeze. Kimmy must have noticed also because she bent down and asked Abigail if she was okay.

"I'm scared," Abigail admitted.

"I'm a little nervous too, so when you get ready to say your lines, look at me first and I will smile at you. And then when it is my turn to say my lines, I will look at you, and you can smile at me."

"Almost like a secret," said Abigail.

"Yes," said Kimmy.

Abigail was so excited to have an almost secret with Kimmy that she didn't even notice the queasy feeling in her tummy was gone. She looked at Kimmy a couple of times and practiced her smile.

When it was time for the curtain to rise and the play to begin, Miss Iris moved to the left of the stage and stood behind the curtain where the children could see her but the audience could not. Each child recited his or her lines about daily servings, vitamins, and minerals with an enthusiasm that is rarely found when talking about the subject of nutrition. When Tommy and Abigail recited their poem about carrots and healthy eyesight, applause rang out loud and long, and it seemed to them that practically everyone in town was in the auditorium that night.

When it was all over, everyone helped themselves to granola bars and fruit punch provided by the town council members. The twins, no longer dressed as carrots, stood by their parents munching on their snacks.

"Going to school is the bestest thing ever," said Abigail to no one in particular.

"Yeah," agreed Tommy as he drank his third glass of punch. "I think so too."

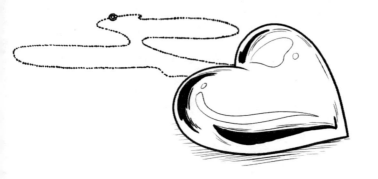

The Locket

Kimmy Curlytail usually went to school early
to play with her friends, but on this particular
day, she stood in front of Albertson's five-
and-dime store admiring a little silver locket
that was displayed prominently in the store
window. The locket was in the shape of a
small heart and hung on a delicate silver
chain. It was the most beautiful thing she

had ever seen. *It must be new*, she thought to herself.

She stood there so long gazing at the lovely locket that she was almost late for school. As the school bell rang out, Kimmy began to run. Thankfully, the school was only two blocks from the store, and Kimmy was a very fast runner.

All morning long Kimmy dreamed about what it would be like to wear the locket. It would look wonderful with the fancy white dress she got for her birthday. She could picture all the other girls admiring her and asking, "Wherever did you get such a beautiful necklace?" She was so caught up in her daydreaming that she didn't even notice the other children had all gone outside for lunch and recess.

"Kimmy," said Miss Iris, "aren't you going to lunch?"

"Oh, yes," said Kimmy, suddenly realizing that the room was empty. She then grabbed her sack lunch and quickly went out to join the others.

That night at the supper table, Kimmy told her mom all about the locket. "It sounds very lovely, dear," Ma Curlytail said as she passed the mashed potatoes to Jimmy. "I'm sure some little girl will be extremely pleased to receive such a gift." Kimmy, holding a fork full of corn midway to her mouth, looked at her mother in surprise. She hadn't thought about someone else buying or wearing the locket.

"But Ma, I don't want someone else to have it. I want to be the one to wear it," she said with tears in her eyes.

"Well, dear," Ma Curlytail replied, "as much as your Pa and I would like to buy you a locket, it just isn't possible. With such a large family to take care of, there just isn't enough extra money for fancy jewelry." Kimmy didn't argue with Ma, but she ate the rest of her dinner in a sad silence.

As Kimmy lay in bed that night, she thought about what Ma had said. She knew her family wasn't poor because they had a nice house, nice clothes, and plenty to eat. They even took an occasional trip to the ice cream parlor. But Kimmy still wished that her parents had enough money to buy her that locket. "If I didn't have six brothers, I could have all the lockets I wanted," Kimmy mumbled to herself. But deep down, Kimmy was very fond of all her brothers. Johnny always carried her bucket into the house after they picked apples. Jimmy and Jaimie had worked a paper route for the whole summer so they could buy her that fancy white dress. Jared read her bedtime stories. Jason had built a small bed for her doll. And Justin had once offered her his paper clip collection. She drifted off to sleep thinking of all the nice things her brothers did for her.

Kimmy slept well that night and had forgotten all about the locket until she arrived at school the next morning. Much to her amazement, Alice Redfeather stood on the playground near the swings showing Betsy Woolrich the very locket that had been in Albertson's window the day before. As Kimmy approached, Betsy turned and said, "Hi, Kimmy. Look at Alice's new locket."

"It's very nice," Kimmy said in a voice barely above a whisper.

Kimmy felt absolutely miserable the rest of the day, so much, in fact, that she didn't even join the rest of the children in their fun and games during recess. On the way home from school that afternoon, she even said something mean to her brother Jason, which was totally unlike the loving Kimmy everyone usually knew. As the week went by, Kimmy finally returned to her normal loving and cheerful self.

About a month later, on a sunless, dreary Wednesday, Kimmy saw something shiny lying in the dirt near the slide. As she bent over to take a closer look, she gasped in surprise. There in the dust was Alice's beautiful heart locket. Kimmy quickly picked it up and carefully wiped it clean. In her hand, the tiny heart locket on the delicate silver chain seemed even more beautiful than before.

Kimmy looked around for Alice, who was standing near the back door of the schoolhouse talking with Sammie Gruff. She then looked back down at the locket in her hand. Alice didn't seem to notice the missing locket, so Kimmy thought maybe she would just hang on to it for a while longer before giving it back. She wanted to see what she would look like with the necklace on. She wanted to see if it would look as great as she had imagined. Kimmy hid the locket in the pocket of her dress and kept playing until the bell rang.

As Kimmy worked on her long division, she smiled and gave her pocket an occasional pat. At first, Kimmy felt happy just knowing that she was in possession of the locket for a short while, but then she began to feel guilty for not giving the locket back to Alice as soon as she had found it. Kimmy knew that it was wrong to keep things that weren't hers. However, by the time school let out for the day, Kimmy's desire to keep the locket had grown stronger than her guilt. So much so that she completely ignored the sight of Alice frantically looking around her desk area.

When Kimmy reached home that afternoon, she ran straight past Ma without even giving her a hug. She ran up the stairs and down the hall to the bathroom, where she hurriedly locked the door. Kimmy took the locket from its hiding place in her pocket and carefully fastened it around her neck. As she looked in the mirror, a small squeal of delight escaped her lips. Just then, Jaimie banged on the door. "Hurry up, sis," he said. "I need to use the toilet."

"I'll be right out," Kimmy said in a nervous voice.

She took off the necklace and put it back into her pocket. She then flushed the toilet and washed her hands so her brother wouldn't ask her what she had been doing in the bathroom.

That night as Kimmy lay in her comfortable feather bed, the feeling of guilt was back in the pit of her stomach. She tried hard to rationalize the feeling away. "Well," she said to the picture of Granny and Grandpa Curlytail that hung over her dresser, "It's not like I stole the locket. And anyways, Alice has lots of other nice jewelry." Having said that, she rolled over and fell into a troubled sleep.

The next morning Kimmy ate her pancakes in haste, kissed Ma good-bye, and ran out the door without waiting for any of her brothers. She practically ran all the way to school. Once she was there, she sat behind a group of bushes at the far edge of the playground.

Confident that no one could see her, she took out the troublesome heart locket and just stared at it. As she did, she noticed something that she hadn't seen before. On the side of the locket was a tiny latch. Kimmy ever so gently opened the locket, revealing two small portraits. The picture on the left was of a handsome male turkey looking quite dapper in his tuxedo and top hat, and the picture on the right was of a beautiful young female turkey in a white satin gown. Kimmy began to cry. What she held in her hand were portraits of Alice's mother and father, who had gone to heaven when Alice was small. Kimmy knew this was the reason why Alice lived with her older sister Henrietta Redfeather, Fern Valley's assistant librarian.

Fresh guilt washed over Kimmy. To her, it was just a beautiful piece of jewelry, but to Alice, it must mean so much more. "It's a way to keep her ma and pa close to her heart," whispered Kimmy. At that moment, Kimmy knew what to do. She must give the locket back to Alice at once. As Kimmy crawled out from her hiding spot, she spied Alice sitting alone on the back steps of the little red schoolhouse.

But as Kimmy began to head toward Alice, the school bell rang, announcing the start of the new school day. All of the children poured into the classroom and found their seats. Their teacher, Miss Iris, stood by her desk ready to pass back the homework she had graded the previous night. Before she could do so, Kimmy raised her hand.

"Yes, Kimmy," Miss Iris said with a smile.

"I have something important I need to tell Alice."

"Can't it wait until recess?"

"No," said Kimmy in a bit firmer voice.

"Very well then."

Kimmy then stood in front of the entire classroom and explained how she had been jealous of Alice, how she had found the locket, and how she had kept it. She walked over to where Alice was seated and handed her the locket. "I'm sorrier than I can ever say, and I hope you can forgive me."

"Of course," said Alice, who was thrilled to have her locket back once again. Kimmy breathed a sigh of relief as she sat back down. She knew that she would never again keep something that didn't belong to her.

The Campout

It was June, school was out, and Roberta and Mildred Cornstalk were looking forward to the special sleepover Mama and Papa Cornstalk said they could have. They were going to set up the tent in the backyard and invite some friends to join them. There would be a campfire supervised by Papa and a picnic packed by Mama. The girls were extremely excited.

"How many friends may we invite?" Mildred asked her mother.

"Oh, I imagine two friends each would be acceptable," she replied.

"I want to invite Sammie Gruff and Alice Redfeather," said Roberta. "I bet they've never been on a campout before because they live in town."

"Then I will invite Betsy Woolrich and Kimmy Curlytail," Mildred said as she crazily hopped from one foot to the other.

The girls spent a pleasant afternoon calling their friends to invite them over. The Super Duper Campout, as the occasion had been dubbed, was to occur on Friday. All four of the invited guests had received permission, and everyone was supposed to arrive at the Cornstalks' home by five o'clock.

"This is going to be the best campout ever," said Mildred as she and Roberta rummaged in the hall closet for sleeping bags.

"I agree," said Roberta.

The girls soon found four sleeping bags, which would be enough for themselves, Alice, and Sammie. Betsy and Kimmy were each going to bring their own bags. All that was left to do was to help Papa carry firewood to the fire pit out back, where the tent was already set up.

Friday morning arrived, and the day promised to be clear and sunny. The girls began eating their French toast, but between bites they pestered Mama Cornstalk to know what she was going to pack for their picnic.

"Well," said Mama, "I thought I would make some fresh corn fritters. Then I thought I would pack some of those little sweet pickles that Alice likes, black olives, apples, cheddar cheese, milk, and of course marshmallows for roasting."

"Of course," said Mildred.

"An absolute must," added Roberta, whose laughter was soon joined by Mama's and Mildred's.

The girls were even more thrilled when they learned that their little brother, Edward, was going to spend the night with Kimmy's six brothers, Johnny, Jimmy, Jaimie, Jared, Jason, and Justin. A sleepover was always better without a pesky little brother trying to snoop and pry into everything. And besides, they knew Edward would have a good time as well. He might be a pesky brother, but Roberta and Mildred were still quite fond of him.

Five o'clock sharp found all four invited guests on the Cornstalk front porch, eager with anticipation. Betsy and Kimmy each carried a sleeping bag and an overnight bag with her toothbrush, pajamas, and a set of clean clothes. Alice and Sammie just held their overnight bags, but Sammie's bag contained an extra treat. Her mother had packed a bag of chocolate-covered raisins for the girls to share.

Roberta and Mildred invited everyone into the living room where they all chattered at once. Just then, Mama entered the room with a large flashlight and the picnic basket. "Why don't you girls all grab a sleeping bag and your things and take them out to the tent?" she said.

"Okay," said everyone, scrambling quickly.

As they trudged outside, arms bulging with their load, they were met by Papa Cornstalk, who was carrying lawn chairs to the fire pit. He pointed to the tent and told them to deposit their belongings.

When the girls finally had their sleeping bags arranged inside the tent and their overnight bags neatly placed at the end of each one, they climbed out and sat down. Mama handed Roberta the flashlight and asked her to put it close to the door of the tent in case someone had to get up in the night to go to the bathroom.

"I will leave the back porch light on as well," she added.

The six excited girls now looked to Mama and Papa to see what was going to happen next. Papa immediately took charge. "We each need to find a long thin stick from the woods for roasting our marshmallows. And when everybody has found one, I will sharpen the ends with my pocket knife."

Soon everyone had a sharpened stick, and it was time to eat the picnic supper that Mama had spread out on the picnic table. Everyone piled their plates high and waited for Papa to bless the food. After Papa's short but thankful prayer, everyone dug in.

"These corn fritters are really good, Mrs. Cornstalk," said Sammie.

"Why thank you, Sammie," said a very pleased Mama.

"These pickles are good too," said Alice.

Mama just laughed because everyone knew that Alice absolutely loved pickles. Alice liked pickles so much that her sister Henrietta jokingly called her Little Pickle.

"Well," said Papa after they were all finished, "if we are going to roast marshmallows, we had better get the fire started."

Soon Papa had a roaring fire going, and Mama was passing out the marshmallows. Each girl's sharpened stick worked really well for stabbing the sugary treats, but it turned out that everyone had a different method for roasting. Roberta found a nice spot with hot coals and no flames to roast hers, and she methodically turned the marshmallow over and over until it was browned to golden perfection. Mildred thrust hers into the flames, catching it on fire. She then blew it out and popped the blackened mass into her mouth.

"That's gross," said Sammie, who was managing to roast hers over the flames but without catching it on fire.

Kimmy, who seemed too impatient to really roast hers, ate it practically in its original state. Alice, for some unknown reason, squashed hers flat before roasting it. Mildred, who was now on her second flaming marshmallow, tried to blow it out, but the darn thing refused to cooperate. She began to wave it around trying to put it out.

"Stop that," screamed Alice, who was standing next to her. "You are going to catch me on fire."

Mildred thought it was funny, so she waved the burning sugar at Alice once more. "Mildred Ann," said Papa in a stern voice. Everyone stopped what they were doing and looked at Papa. "We do not play with fire because it can be very dangerous. What if you would have burnt Alice? Also, we do not annoy our special friends."

"Yes, Papa," Mildred said. She then turned to Alice and said she was sorry. She knew Papa never tolerated behavior that was rude or actions that were dangerous. Papa was especially concerned with fire safety because when he was young, he knew a boy who burnt down a barn while playing with matches.

"Okay, everyone, it's time to go into the house and get ready for bed," Mama Cornstalk announced.

"Can we tell stories when we come back out?" asked Mildred in a nervous voice. She always felt funny when she did something wrong.

"For a little while."

Mildred let out the breath she had been holding. She could tell everything was fine again. Mama and Papa were usually fair and quick to forgive.

So the six girls grabbed their pajamas and toothbrushes from the tent and trooped up to Mildred and Roberta's bedroom. After they were ready, they all raced back to the campfire.

"Who wants to tell the first story?" asked Papa once all the girls were safely seated around the fire.

"I do, I do," said the usually quiet Sammie, much to everyone's amazement.

"You all know my Uncle Cyrus," she began. And of course, everyone did, because Uncle Cyrus was not only the oldest goat in Fern Valley but was also the local mail carrier. She then proceeded to tell about the time Uncle Cyrus fell on the birthday cake at his seventy-fifth birthday celebration. By the time she was finished, everyone was laughing so hard they were crying.

When each girl had told her story, they headed for the tent. Mama tucked each girl into her sleeping bag with a hug and a kiss while Papa put out the fire.

"Goodnight, Mama," said Roberta and Mildred.

"Goodnight, Mrs. Cornstalk," said Kimmy, Betsy, Sammie, and Alice.

"Goodnight, girls," said Mama. "Sleep well."

And with that, six happy and tired girls were lulled to sleep by the sound of crickets gently making their cricket music underneath the light of the moon.

The Bike

It was shiny chrome and candy apple red with a white basket and a squeaker horn. It was absolutely the best bike Sammie Gruff had ever seen. As she stood there admiring the new bike at the end of the ladder aisle in Mr. Flock's hardware store, she could already imagine herself riding it down the main street. Sammie had a dream that she had never told anyone, and that was to own a brand new girl's bike.

Sammie had an old bike that had been handed down to her from a cousin. But it was a boy's bike with no basket and lots of dings and scrapes. It wasn't that she was ungrateful for the bike. Sammie was always the most grateful and pleasant goat you could find in Fern Valley. Any of her friends would tell you so. It was just that she had never had a brand new bike before.

"It's so beautiful," she said under her breath.

Mr. Flock, who was walking past with a box of new hammers, set them down and began scratching behind his wooly, black head. He was wondering where he was going to put them. "What did you say, dear?"

Sammie just looked at the floor, but Mr. Flock had already forgotten he had even asked her a question. Mr. Flock was like that. He was one of the nicest sheep you could ever meet and an extremely fair merchant, but he was easily distracted.

Sammie took one more look at the bike before heading for home. Four blocks down from the hardware store and three more blocks to the left was Sammie's home. It was a beautiful Victorian house with stained-glass windows and an enormous front porch. As she let herself in the front door, she could hear her mother singing in the kitchen.

Sammie's mother, Martha, was in the same choir as Betsy Woolrich's grandmother and could often be found singing hymns as she cooked, cleaned, or just sat relaxing. It always made Sammie feel warm and happy inside to hear her mother sing joyfully to the Lord.

Sammie went into the kitchen and sat down at the table. Her mother was putting a noodle casserole in the oven, so she didn't see or hear Sammie come in. When she turned around, she let out a startled noise. "Hello, muffin; I didn't hear you come in. So what have you been up to this fine summer day?"

"Well," Sammie said a bit hesitantly, "I was at the hardware store, and I saw the most beautiful bike ever made."

"Really? And what made this particular bike so beautiful?"

Sammie spent the next ten minutes explaining the beauties of the bike: its shiny chrome, its perfect color, the useful basket, its newness, and the fact that it was made for a girl. Her hesitancy turned to excitement as she explained the dream she had to own such a bike.

"I see," said her mother. "Well, let's discuss it when Daddy comes home from work."

It was another hour before Mr. Gruff got home and they sat down to dinner. As her mother scooped generous helpings of noodle casserole and green beans onto each plate, Sammie told her father all about the bike.

"Since you already had your birthday last month, perhaps we could come to some sort of an agreement if you really want this bike."

"Oh yes, Daddy." Sammie nodded eagerly.

"You might want to wait until you hear the bargain," he said and then laughed. Mr. Gruff agreed to pay for half of the bike if Sammie would pay for the other half. This meant that she would have to do extra chores around the house and neighborhood to earn enough money.

Since the bike sold for forty dollars, she needed twenty dollars to pay for her half. She had seven dollars left from her birthday, so that meant she had to come up with another thirteen dollars. She thought that should be a cinch. Well, she hoped it would a cinch. She noticed Mrs. Rocky, the elderly goat who lived next door, had a lot of weeds in her flower garden. Maybe in the morning she would see if Mrs. Rocky needed help weeding.

Sammie was awake with the sun the next morning, and after quickly dressing and practically inhaling a bowl of cereal, she was out the door. She rang Mrs. Rocky's doorbell and patiently waited. When Mrs. Rocky answered the door, she invited her in.

"It's so good to see you, dear," she said.

"It's nice to see you too, Mrs. Rocky," Sammie said politely.

"And what are you up to this summer?"

"Well," said Sammie, who was suddenly attacked with a case of shyness, "I was wondering if you had any odd jobs that I could do, like weeding. I'm trying to save money for a new bike."

Mrs. Rocky smiled encouragingly at Sammie. "As a matter of fact, dear, I could really use some help weeding the flowers. I could also use some help cleaning out the attic. You know, I'm not as young as I used to be."

So after a few instructions, Sammie got busy weeding. Mrs. Rocky had a large lot with several flowerbeds, so it took Sammie the better part of the morning and afternoon to finish the weeding. After she was done, they agreed that the attic would have to wait until the next day.

"Mother, Mrs. Rocky paid me two dollars for weeding her flowers." Sammie excitedly waved the bills around.

"That's wonderful, dear," her mother said as she added some pepper to the black bean soup she was making. "How much more do you need?"

"I only need eleven more dollars. And tomorrow I am going to help Mrs. Rocky clean out her attic."

"Well, that should be quite interesting. I don't think Mrs. Rocky has cleaned out that attic for at least twenty years."

Sammie's mother was right. Mrs. Rocky's attic was crammed full of odds and ends of things. In one corner stood several tall dressers with old clothes peeking out of the overstuffed drawers, and in the other corner were all manner of lamps, baby strollers, tricycles, plant pots, pictures, and boxes. Everything was covered in a fine layer of dust, which made Mrs. Rocky and Sammie start to sneeze. "Why don't you begin by opening those two windows," said Mrs. Rocky.

They spent the whole day dusting, sorting, and organizing. One pile was to be picked up by the thrift store man, one pile was to be given to Mrs. Rocky's grandchildren, and one pile was for the trash barrel. Sammie began carrying the trash pile down an armload at a time. By the time the two of them finished the attic, Sammie was one dirty, hungry, and tired goat.

"You've done a fine job, Sammie," said Mrs. Rocky as she handed her a ten-dollar bill.

Sammie could hardly believe it. She had never earned ten whole dollars before. She hugged Mrs. Rocky so hard she almost toppled the woman over. This meant she would only need to earn one more dollar. Sammie thanked Mrs. Rocky again and headed home to show her mother.

As she lay in bed that night, Sammie wondered what she could do to earn that last dollar. Nothing came to mind immediately, so she just said her prayers and went to sleep.

The next morning when her father learned she only needed one more dollar, he asked if she wanted to help him wash the car.

"Oh, yes, Daddy. Thank you very much."

Sammie was eager to earn her last dollar, but she also wanted to do a good job for her daddy, so she took her time. Her father washed and rinsed the high parts, and Sammie washed and rinsed the low parts and the wheels. Finally they were done, and Sammie had enough for her half of the bike purchase.

"Can we go to the hardware store now?" she asked her father.

"Yes, muffin, I just need to grab my keys and wallet from the house."

Sammie was already in the car waiting when her father returned. He just smiled and got in the car. Sammie, who was usually pretty quiet, chatted all the way to Mr. Flock's. Once there, she quickly found Mr. Flock and told him she wanted to purchase the bike. As she counted out her twenty dollars and added it to the twenty her father had already set on the counter, Sammie felt a wonderful sense of accomplishment. Not only would she be the owner of the most beautiful girl's bike ever made, she had also worked hard to earn it, and that felt really good.

"I'll see you at home," she told her father as she mounted her new bike outside of the hardware store.

"Okay, muffin. Have a good ride home."

"I will, Daddy." Her father smiled, knowing that she would.

The Proposal

Alice Redfeather loved her sister dearly. After all, her sister was the only family she had left since her parents died in an accident. But Alice just could not understand what Henrietta saw in George Gobbler. George was ordinary. George was always acting nervous around Henrietta. George was a guy.

"Alice, are you ready?" Henrietta said from the next room.

"Yes, Henrietta. I'm coming." Alice walked slowly to the living room, where her sister and George were waiting. The three of them were going on a picnic at Green Meadow Park. It was obvious from Alice's actions that she was less then thrilled with the idea of spending time with George. But Henrietta didn't seem to notice.

"Finally," Henrietta said. "Let's get going." Alice and Henrietta only lived four blocks from the park, so they all walked. George carried the picnic basket full of corn salad sandwiches, dainty chocolate éclairs, celery sticks, napkins, and cups. Henrietta carried a blanket to sit on, and Alice carried a thermos of lemonade.

When they arrived at the park, Alice saw Sammie. "May I go play?"

"Yes, dear," her sister replied absentmindedly.

Alice set the thermos down and headed for the bench where Sammie was sitting. Alice could tell that Sammie had been feeding the pigeons because she was holding an empty paper sack and there were still breadcrumbs on the ground.

"Hi, Alice. What are you doing here?"

"I'm on a picnic with George and Henrietta," Alice said dejectedly.

"That sounds nice. I love to go on picnics!"

"So do I, but it would be way better if George didn't have to go everywhere with us. This is the third time in four days that he has been to see Henrietta. I just wish she would tell him to get lost."

"What's wrong with George?" asked Sammie. "I think he's kind of cute."

"He's nice looking, I guess. But I think he's boring." Deep down, Alice knew this wasn't the real problem. The real problem was that she was afraid. Before Henrietta met George, all of her time and attention were focused on Alice. After she met George, everything changed.

Sammie and Alice played on the swings, the jungle gym, and the slide for about an hour before Sammie had to go home.

"I told my mom I would help her pick pears today, so I really need to get going."

"All right, I'll see you later." Alice waved good-bye to Sammie until she was out of sight.

Alice then walked back to where Henrietta had spread out the blanket. George was talking quietly to her. Alice couldn't hear what he was saying, but judging from the look on Henrietta's face, she was sure she wasn't going to like it

"Oh, there you are, Alice. George and I have something wonderful to tell you."

Alice had a sudden sick feeling in her stomach. *Don't say it; please don't say it*, she thought. Alice knew what was coming, and she did not want to hear it.

"George has asked me to marry him," Henrietta said. She was looking at George so lovingly that she didn't see the angry look on Alice's face.

"You can't get married to George. It will wreck everything. He's just a big dork always hanging around us."

Henrietta turned in shock to look at Alice. Alice looked at the ground in shame. She had never been so rude to her sister before. She had never been that rude to anyone before. She knew she should apologize, but the words just seemed to stick in her throat. Suddenly Alice turned and ran for home.

Once home, she went to her bedroom, flopped on the bed, and began to cry. *Why does everything have to change?* she thought. A few minutes later, she heard a knock.

"May I come in?" said Henrietta from the doorway.

"Yes."

Henrietta sat down beside Alice and gently stroked her head. "What happened out there just now?"

Instead of answering the question, Alice asked, "Where's George?"

"I sent him home because I think we need to talk."

Alice started crying again. "I'm so sorry I said those mean things at the park."

Henrietta remained silent, waiting for Alice to tell her what was really wrong. After a few minutes, it all came tumbling out. Alice explained that she thought Henrietta wouldn't want to be responsible for her anymore if she married George. She thought that Henrietta wouldn't have time to love her and care for her because she would be loving and caring for George. And what would George think about the situation? Would he think Alice was too loud or her room too messy? Would he get upset if she left the orange juice out or forgot to put away her shoes?

"And if you marry George, will we have to sell our house?"

Henrietta hugged Alice tightly. "Love isn't like that, honey. My heart has room for both you and George. And George loves you too. He wants us to be a family, and he wants us to all live together. If he didn't, I don't think he would be someone I could fall in love with and promise to marry. And as far as the house is concerned, George will move in with us."

Alice thought about that for a moment and decided that maybe the addition of George to their lives wouldn't be so bad after all. "Do you think we could call George and ask him back over? After all, we never did eat our lunch."

"I think that would be a great idea. I'll go call him right now."

George was more than happy to come back over. On the phone, Henrietta explained to him what the problem had been, and he was eager to reassure Alice that she and Henrietta were a package deal. George was from a large, loving family, and he hoped to have a large family himself. He thought Alice and Henrietta would be a great start on making that dream come true.

"I'm sorry for the mean things I said," Alice told George when he arrived.

George gave her a hug and said he understood. "Now let's get back to having some fun. I think we have a picnic to finish." So they all walked back to the park. Henrietta spread the blanket out, George rummaged through the basket until he found the cups, and Alice poured each of them a glass of lemonade. They all laughed when George got out the paper plates because they started to blow away before Henrietta could put the sandwiches on them.

A few days later, Alice saw Sammie at the park again. "Hey, Sammie."

"Hi, Alice. I was hoping there would be someone here to hang out with."

Alice laughed and said, "Me too."

"So how did your picnic go the other day?"

Alice blushed, remembering how she had almost ruined the picnic with her insecurities and fears. She told Sammie everything. She told her how she had spoken rudely, how Henrietta had reassured her, and how George had come back so they could start over. "He's really quite nice once you get to know him. And he says that Henrietta and I are a package deal. He comes from a big family, you know. That means that when he marries Henrietta I will have a grandma, a grandpa, and lots of aunts and uncles."

"Wow, that's pretty cool."

"I think so too," said Alice cheerfully. And the two girls went off to swing.

The Sitter

It was a cold and rainy Wednesday when Mama Bigpaw received the call from her mother, who lived in Pleasant Meadows, the next town over. She cheerily picked up the receiver. "Hello, Mrs. Bigpaw speaking."

"Hello, dear," said Mother Hopsy. "I hope I didn't interrupt anything important."

"Of course not, Mother. I was just ironing the children's clothes."

Mother Hopsy went on to explain that the reason for her call was to invite Mrs. Bigpaw to hear Annie VonGoosekin speak about gardening. "I know this is short notice, my dear, but I just found out about it this morning. Is there any way you can find a sitter for the children so you could attend with me?"

"I don't know, Mother," she said while quickly trying to think of whom she could ask. "Let me call around, and I will get back with you."

"That's fine, sweetie; talk with you later."

It was known far and wide that Mrs. Bigpaw loved to garden, and from time to time she even wrote articles for the *Fern Valley Gazette*. So it was no surprise that she wanted to go and hear her favorite author speak about the hobby she adored so much. But who could she call on such short notice?

"I know," she said to herself, "I shall call Mrs. Sharpbeak." Mrs. Sharpbeak was an elderly chicken who lived three houses down from the Bigpaws. Earlier in the summer, she had offered to watch the twins should the need ever arise.

Mrs. Bigpaw dialed the number and waited. The phone rang about four times before Mrs. Sharpbeak finally answered. "Hello," she said, followed by some heavy breathing.

"Hello, Mrs. Sharpbeak, are you okay?"

"Of course, dear. I was just putting some things away in the basement when the phone started ringing. I'm not a spring chicken anymore, you know, so the stairs made me a bit winded." Mrs. Sharpbeak cackled at her own joke.

Mrs. Bigpaw laughed too and then began to tell about her mother's offer. "And so I was wondering if you would be able to watch the children till five o'clock, when Mr. Bigpaw gets home from the newspaper office?"

"Not a problem, dear," said Mrs. Sharpbeak. "Send them right over."

Mrs. Bigpaw hung up the phone and went to find the children. She found them both in the living room looking glumly out the window. "Children, you are going to stay with Mrs. Sharpbeak until you father gets home from work."

"How come?" said the twins in unison.

"Grandma Hopsy called and invited me over to hear a guest speaker, and I must leave right away if I am to get there in time," she said excitedly. The children looked even glummer, if that was possible.

"I don't want to go to Mrs. Sharpbeak's house," said Tommy.

"Neither do I," said Abigail.

Mrs. Bigpaw looked surprised. "Why ever not?"

Abigail let Tommy answer. "She won't be any fun. She's too old!"

Mrs. Bigpaw frowned. "Being old doesn't mean a person isn't fun. Now go get ready please."

So the children slowly walked to the closet to get their rain boots and jackets. When they were ready, they followed Mrs. Bigpaw down the street to Mrs. Sharpbeak's house, grumbling under their breath the whole way. Minutes later, they arrived and stood on the large front porch supported by large white pillars. Before rapping on the door sharply with the strong metal door knocker, Mrs. Bigpaw raised one eyebrow and looked at the children warningly. They understood without words that their mother expected them to be on their best behavior.

Mrs. Sharpbeak opened the heavy oak door and bid them entrance. The children looked into the great drawing room curiously. The room was full of antique tables, chairs, bookcases, and all manner of other interesting items. Long red velvet draperies tied back with gold braided cords hung jauntily in the windows. Expensive Persian rugs covered the oak floor, looking as fresh as they had when they were purchased thirty years before. But the most amazing thing in the room was the large chandelier that hung from the twelve-foot ceiling. It contained no less than 240 Austrian crystal prisms, and when the sun shone just right, tiny rainbows danced on the walls like miniature ballerinas.

"Come in, come in," she said, closing the door behind them. "I am especially glad to have company today because it is gingerbread Tuesday."

Abigail turned to look at Mrs. Sharpbeak. "What is gingerbread Tuesday?"

"Well, you see, dear, every Tuesday since my children were small, I have been baking gingerbread cake. And although my children and grandchildren are all grown now, baking has become such a habit I can't seem to stop. So today the two of you can help me eat it up

so I won't have to eat it all week by myself."
Abigail and Tommy both grinned from ear to
ear.

The children wandered around looking at
each and every object in the great drawing
room as Mrs. Sharpbeak and Mrs. Bigpaw said
their good-byes. "And Mr. Bigpaw will pick
the children up at about ten after five," they
heard their mother say.

"No problem, dear. Go and have a good
time." Mrs. Sharpbeak called everyone
dear, even Uncle Cyrus. Everyone in town
found this really quite funny because Uncle
Cyrus was at least ten years older than Mrs.
Sharpbeak.

Mrs. Sharpbeak turned and looked at the
children. "Well, children, are you ready for
some cake?"

"Yes, ma'am," said both children
somewhat more cheerfully than they had
spoken to their mother only moments before.
Stepping aside so Mrs. Sharpbeak could lead

the way, they silently followed her. They all walked down the wide hall toward the back of the house until they reached what the twins thought must be the biggest kitchen in the whole world. It wasn't full of antiques like the drawing room but was much homier with its six-foot-long butcher block table and white-painted chairs. Canisters full of everything imaginable could be seen through the shiny glass panes of the numerous kitchen cabinets, and a large collection of cookie jars lined the countertop.

The smell of cake hung heavy in the air, causing Tommy's stomach to grumble loudly. Mrs. Sharpbeak laughed. "I guess I had better hurry and get that cake served." She then proceeded to slice three very large pieces, which she put on dainty flowered plates. To this she added three glasses of ice-cold milk. And to top it all off, she put huge dollops of whipped cream on everyone's piece of cake.

"This is the best cake," said Tommy, who had begun to eat as soon as the plate was set in front of him.

"It is," agreed Abigail, who ate much more slowly, enjoying every bite thoroughly.

"Why, thank you, children." Mrs. Sharpbeak smiled, and she too began to eat her cake.

"Now then, whatever shall we do today?" she said after they had all finished and the dishes were clean and put away. Abigail and Tommy wanted to see what might be hiding in the old shed out back. "I'm afraid it's just too damp outside to be rooting around that old shed. Why don't we play a game instead?"

"What kind of game?" asked Tommy in a voice that indicated any games Mrs. Sharpbeak owned were probably boring.

"Let's just go and see what I have in the closet." Mrs. Sharpbeak led the way back down the wide hall. She stopped suddenly and opened a door the children hadn't seen on the way to the kitchen. It was a closet with shelves from floor to ceiling, and they were all full of games.

The children peeked in and saw games of every kind. There were card games like Old Maid and Rook. There were checkers and chess, Monopoly and Yahtzee. There were tins that held marbles and jacks and tiddly winks. Pin the Tail on the Donkey was on the very top shelf, and Chinese checkers was on the bottom shelf. There was a box containing an erector set and one long can that held pick-up sticks. But it was the middle two shelves that caught Abigail's attention because they were full of puzzles.

She squealed in delight, "Can we put a puzzle together?"

Mrs. Sharpbeak looked in Tommy's direction to see if he was interested in a puzzle as well. Tommy nodded his head, and the three of them began to search through the pile. They finally decided on a picture of a train going over a trestle bridge in the middle of winter.

Mrs. Sharpbeak found a card table and three folding chairs in the basement, which Tommy and Abigail helped her carry to the drawing room. "This way if we don't finish the puzzle before your father comes we can leave it set out until you are able to come back." The children thought that was a marvelous idea.

Mrs. Sharpbeak and the children began by turning all the pieces face up. Then they found all the edge pieces and began to work on putting the border together. With all three of them working diligently, it took less than a half an hour for the border to be finished.

"I will work on finding train pieces," said Tommy confidently.

Abigail, not to be outdone by her brother, looked the puzzle over carefully. "Then I will find the green pine tree pieces." That left Mrs. Sharpbeak to work on a snow-covered section in the bottom right-hand corner.

After about an hour the puzzle was beginning to shape up nicely. The children would have continued working without stopping except that Abigail noticed Mrs. Sharpbeak was sort of stretching her back and wings. "Should we take a break?" she asked.

"Why yes, dear, that is a good idea. Why don't I go and get us all some lemonade?"

"May we drink it on the back porch?" asked Abigail. She wanted to try out the lovely porch swing she had seen there.

"I don't see why not."

Once the lemonade was poured and the glasses were set on a small wooden tray, Mrs. Sharpbeak motioned for Tommy to carry them out to the back porch. She held the back screen door open for him and then checked to see that Abigail was following. Tommy set the tray down on one of the wicker end tables and helped himself to a glass. Abigail took the other two and handed one to Mrs. Sharpbeak. The three of them rocked and drank and talked of things like butterflies and apple trees. And that is how Mr. Bigpaw found them when he arrived.

"Well, hello," said Mrs. Sharpbeak in surprise. "Is it after five o'clock already?"

"Yes, ma'am." Mr. Bigpaw explained that he had come around to the back because no one had heard him at the front.

The children reluctantly got up to go home. It was hard for them to tear themselves away from Mrs. Sharpbeak because they had come to realize she was a very interesting person.

"Maybe you can come back tomorrow and we will finish the puzzle," said Mrs. Sharpbeak.

Both children hugged and squeezed her good-bye and began to follow their father home. Suddenly Abigail turned and ran back. "You are more than a sitter," she whispered. "You are like family." And she gave Mrs. Sharpbeak one last hug.

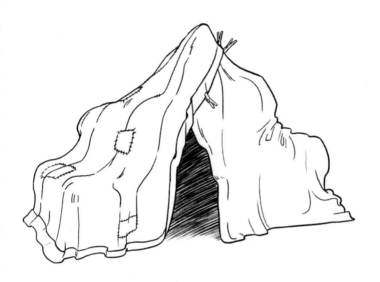

The Fort

Roberta and Mildred Cornstalk were born planners. In their short lives, they had planned a tea club, a campout, and numerous other activities, all of which were great successes. Their latest plan involved a weekend bike ride with their friends.

Saturday morning arrived, and the two excited girls got out of bed and ran to look out the window. Mildred moved the pink, ruffled curtain gently out of the way. "Oh no, it's raining." All of the careful plans they had made to go bike riding with their friends quickly vanished.

The two girls wandered dejectedly down to the kitchen, where their younger brother, Edward, was munching on some oatmeal and toast. Edward looked up with his mouth still full of food. "Hey!"

"Oooh, that's gross," said Roberta. Edward just smiled.

Mama, who was busy at the kitchen sink peeling potatoes for vegetable soup, looked at Edward. "Please don't talk with food in your mouth. And Roberta, will you please hand me those green beans over there on the counter?"

Mildred started pouring herself some cornflakes. When she was finished, she looked out the kitchen window, hoping the rain would stop. Steadily the rain continued to pour and did not look like it would quit any time soon. "Do you want cornflakes too?" she asked Roberta.

"Yeah, I don't feel like oatmeal this morning."

As the three children sat finishing their breakfast, the phone began to ring. "Would one of you get that, please?" Mama asked. "I am in the middle of peeling carrots." Roberta was closest, so she got up.

Picking up the receiver, she spoke into the phone. "Hello?"

"Hi. I guess there won't be any bike ride and picnic today," said Kimmy.

"Not unless your bike has oars and an umbrella," Roberta said. "Maybe Mama will let you, Sammie, Alice, and Betsy come over to play in the house instead. Let me ask." Mama didn't mind, so they decided to meet after lunch. Roberta called the other girls and sat back down to finish her cornflakes. She then washed the breakfast dishes for her mother before grabbing her sister by the wing and waltzing her to the living room. "What are we going to do when everyone gets here?" she asked.

Mildred looked as if she was thinking very hard. "I don't know. Maybe we could put puzzles together or we could play a card game."

"That's boring. That's what we always do when it rains."

The two girls sat down on the old green couch and tried to think. Roberta looked around the room, hoping an idea would just pop into her head. And sure enough, when she looked at the pile of lap quilts in the corner, she had a brilliant idea. "We could build an indoor fort!"

Mildred's mind had been wandering, so she looked at Roberta blankly. Roberta pointed to a pile of lap quilts in the corner of the living room and repeated herself. "We could drape them over chairs and stuff. And then when we're done, we could have a picnic."

Mildred, who had finally caught on to what her sister was saying, got excited too. "Yeah, that's a great idea. Do you think Mama will mind?"

"Let's go find out." So the two girls ran back to the kitchen to ask their mother. Mama Cornstalk, who had finished working on her soup and was now making some homemade bread, looked up at the two chattering girls.

"Whoa, slow down, you two. I can't understand a word you are saying."

Mildred nudged Roberta, who began to tell Mama about their big idea. She told her about building a fort in the living room and having an indoor picnic. She even promised that they would put everything back when they were finished and would sweep up any crumbs.

"All right," said Mama, "I think that will be fine. But you must have everything picked up by the time Papa comes in for supper."

"Okay," the girls said in unison and then rushed out of the room.

A little while later, the front doorbell rang. The girls, who had been busy moving the dining room chairs into the living room, answered the door. Kimmy and Betsy were both standing there shaking off umbrellas. "Come in," Mildred said.

"Yes, do," said Roberta, who began to explain what was going on. "I think if we move these two chairs across from the couch and if we put a single chair at each end, we can drape the blankets over the tops and clothespin them together."

The doorbell rang again a few minutes later, and Mildred went to let Sammie and Alice in. Since Sammie's mother had driven both girls over, they both waved good-bye before turning to join the fun.

Edward, tired of playing by himself, also joined the group of girls arranging chairs. "Here, Edward," Roberta said. "Hold this end of the quilt while I drape the other end over the couch. Betsy and Mildred, do the same with that red quilt on the other side. Kimmy and Sammie, you can pin them in the middle, and Alice can hold the clothespins for you." Roberta was a great organizer, and everyone was happy to follow her directions.

When they were all done, everyone stepped back to look at the masterpiece. "It's sort of droopy in the middle," Betsy said. They all nodded their heads in agreement. Suddenly Edward ran off. Moments later he came back with the base and pole from the family's artificial Christmas tree.

"This should do the trick. Hold the quilts up a little, sis," he said, pointing to Mildred. She did what he asked. He then crawled under, put the base in the middle of the floor, and proceeded to attach the pole, creating a teepee effect. The girls were all impressed. Edward tried to pretend it wasn't any big deal, but secretly he was pleased with all of their praise.

The girls decided that they needed cushions to sit on, so they went around the house scrounging up all the spare pillows they could find. Edward decided there was enough room for him to lie on the couch. After they finally got everything settled to their satisfaction, they decided to go see what Mama Cornstalk had available for lunch.

Mama fixed them some peanut butter and jelly sandwiches. She then opened some peaches that she had canned the summer before, got out a bag of potato chips, and poured several glasses of fresh cold milk. "Get the serving tray out of the pantry," she told Mildred.

After asking the blessing for their food, the six girls and Edward happily began eating in the cozy comfort of their fort. Edward had found a large lantern-style flashlight, which he turned on and set near the pole in the middle. As they were eating they noticed that they were casting shadows on the quilts hanging down the sides.

Soon they began making shapes and images on the makeshift walls of the fort. "Look, look," said Kimmy. "I'm making a butterfly."

"Yeah, and look at my heart," said Betsy.

Edward began to laugh creepily. "Well, look at my spider." He kept trying to make it look like his shadow spider was landing on the girls. At first the girls pretended to be scared, but soon everyone was laughing so hard they were almost crying.

They were having so much fun that Roberta didn't even notice when she sat on a potato chip. But Kimmy noticed and pointed to Roberta's rear. This started the children to laughing again. In all the laughing and merriment, jostling and moving, the clothespins began to lose their grip on the quilts, and the whole heap fell on the heads of seven very surprised kids.

As they all found their way out of the tangled mass, Mama entered the room.

"Well, what happened here?"

"Our fort collapsed," said Edward.

"It's about time to clean up anyway," said Mama. "Kimmy's ma just called and said it was time for her to come home and help with the chores."

"Okay," they all answered. Then the cleanup began. The girls folded all the quilts into neat squares, and Roberta put them back in the corner where she had found them. Next they collected up all the clothespins and put back all the pillows they had borrowed. Edward took the Christmas tree pole and base back to the basement and then helped carry all of the chairs back to the dining room. Finally, Roberta found a broom to sweep up the potato chip crumbs. When everything was once again neat and tidy, Betsy and Kimmy gathered up their umbrellas and headed for home. Sammie and Alice decided to wait on the porch for Mrs. Gruff, who pulled up only seconds later.

As Roberta and Mildred waved good-bye to their friends, they noticed that the rain had stopped and the sun was trying to peek over the top of a large cloud. "Well, the rain finally stopped," said Roberta.

Mildred laughed. "But wasn't it a great day, rain and all?"

Roberta smiled and closed the front door. "Yes, it was!" And with that, they went to see if there was anything Mama needed help with before Papa got home.

The Visit

Betsy Woolrich impatiently sat on her grandmother's front porch steps. She had only been waiting there fifteen minutes, but to her it seemed like an hour. She looked expectantly up the road every few minutes, hoping to see Uncle John's truck. He had gone to town to pick up her parents from the bus station.

Her parents had been gone for a whole month since their last visit, so she was extremely excited that they were coming home. She hoped they would stay longer than a day this time.

"When are they going to get here?" she said to herself. Just then she saw Uncle John's beat-up old pickup truck coming down the lane. "Grandma, they're here!" she shouted through the screen door.

"Land sakes, child, I could have heard you if I was in the barn." Betsy just smiled at Grandma Woolrich, who was standing in the doorway taking off her apron. Then she took off down the steps two at a time and ran to the truck, where she yanked the door open.

Mama pulled her into the cab and smothered her with kisses.

"Hey, wait a minute. Save some of those for me," said Papa.

Betsy quickly squirmed out of Mama's grasp and into Papa's lap. She gave him a big hug. "I missed you both so much!"

"We missed you too," said Papa.

Finally everyone got out of the truck and headed for the house. Mama and Papa both gave Grandma Woolrich a big hug while Uncle John carried the luggage into the house. Just then Grandpa came from the direction of the barn, where he had been working on the tractor. He had grease all over his face and hands.

"I'd give you a hug, Dad, but you might want to shower first," said Papa.

"You mean you haven't heard that motor grease is taking the place of lotion now?"

Everyone but Grandma laughed at Grandpa Woolrich's joke. She just swatted him and told him to go get cleaned up.

"Supper is almost finished," Grandma said to Mama, Papa, and Betsy. "So why don't we all go in and get cleaned up."

Once everyone was clean and seated, Grandma Woolrich set the food on the table. She had made turnip greens and blackberry dumplings for the occasion, because that was Papa's favorite meal. Everyone was so hungry that there was hardly any conversation for about five or six minutes. Then Betsy turned toward Mama. "I sure hope you and Papa are staying for more than overnight this time."

"Actually, dear, Papa and I have something to tell you after dinner."

Betsy wondered what it could be as she continued to eat. *Oh no*, she thought. *What if they are leaving again for another month?* The blackberry dumplings that had tasted so good moments before suddenly lost their appeal.

When everyone was finished, Betsy and Mama began to clear the table. Grandma Woolrich got up to help, but Mama told her to go sit down and relax in the living room.

Papa, Uncle John, and Grandpa Woolrich began discussing the broken tractor.

Moments later Betsy heard the front screen door close. She looked at her mother. "I think the men went out to the barn."

Her mother didn't appear concerned as she handed Betsy a plate to rinse. Didn't she know that Betsy was eager to hear what they had to tell her? Didn't she care that Betsy was going out of her mind not knowing how long their visit would last?

"Are you going to rinse that plate or just hold it?" asked Mama. Betsy rinsed the plate and took the silverware Mama was holding. Soon they were done and went to join Grandma in the living room.

Mama sat down on the couch and patted the cushion beside her. "Come tell me what you've been doing this summer."

Betsy told Mama about the campout she had gone to at Roberta and Mildred's house. She told her about roasting marshmallows and sleeping in a tent. She also told her about the time it had rained and all her friends and she had built an indoor fort at the Cornstalks' home.

"It sounds like you have been having a really nice summer."

"Yes, it has been pretty nice," Betsy said but without much enthusiasm.

Mama looked at Betsy a little more closely. "What's wrong?"

"I just was wondering how long you and Papa are going to stay this time."

"We will talk all about that when Papa comes back."

Betsy had to be satisfied with that answer because Mama had begun a conversation with Grandma Woolrich about the garden and how well the summer crops were doing. Grandma began explaining the importance of weeding regularly to maintain healthy vegetables, a subject dear to her heart.

With all the things on Betsy's mind, she was having trouble sitting still. She squirmed in her seat, causing her mother to look her way. Betsy stood up and started to leave the room. "I think I'll go out back and swing."

"That sounds good, dear," said Mama.

Betsy headed out back to the wooden swing set that Grandpa Woolrich and Uncle John had built last summer. It was a beautiful set, and she temporarily forgot her concerns as she admired the bright yellow swing seats and the tall, curly slide.

She sat in the middle swing and began to pump her legs. Higher and higher she went with each stretch. She imagined she could touch the fluffy white clouds floating above. One cloud looked like a big trampoline. Betsy wondered what it would be like to jump on a cloud.

Her daydreams were suddenly interrupted by laughter coming from the barn. She could tell which voice was Papa's because it was deep and rich. This made her smile. She loved Mama and Papa so much. She wished they could stay at home instead of always traveling. It wasn't that she didn't love living with Grandpa and Grandma Woolrich and Uncle John; she just wanted to be with her mama and papa more.

She saw the men come from the barn and walk toward the house. They must be done fixing the tractor. Maybe now Papa and Mama would tell her how long they were going to stay. Betsy jumped from the swing and ran to the house.

She let herself in the back door and went to the living room, where everyone was gathered. Papa grabbed her and squeezed her tight. "Hey, sweetie, your mama and I have something we want to tell you."

"Yes, we actually have something wonderful to tell all of you," said Mama.

Papa got up from the couch and looked at everyone before speaking. "While Mama and I were at the Sunnyvale Ski Lodge, we met a man named Mr. Shorthair. He turned out to be a wealthy businessman. We got talking one night, and when he heard about the sweaters your mama and I make and sell, he asked to see some samples. He ended up buying everything we had in stock and ordered one hundred more. It seems he owns a chain of clothing stores near major ski resorts and mountain lodges and thought our sweaters would make a great addition to his winter clothing line."

"Not only that," said Mama, "he wants us to design a line of knit hats and scarves."

Everyone began talking at once until Papa held up his hand. "The best part of all is that we will be able to stop traveling and stay right here in Fern Valley."

Betsy flew to where Papa was standing and hugged him tightly around the waist. "Really, Papa? Really, truly, and honest?"

"Yes, sweetie."

Betsy started to cry. Mama rose from the couch and gently wiped tears from her eyes. "What's the matter?"

"I was just thinking that this is the best visit ever because it will be the last visit."

Mama smiled, Papa smiled, and Betsy smiled. And then they group hugged the tightest, squeeziest group hug Betsy had ever felt. And boy, did it feel good!

The Accident

The Curlytail family consisted of seven children, which made them the largest family in Fern Valley. People often wondered how Ma and Pa Curlytail managed with so many children. Ma always claimed a household full of children was a gift from God and gifts from God were never burdensome.

So when a freak snowstorm dumped so much snow that school had been canceled that Tuesday, Ma just smiled. The children were all delighted as well because this meant a free day to bundle up and play outside.

"I'm going out to the barn to see if Pa needs help chopping firewood," Johnny said to Ma.

"Okay, sweetie. And tell Pa I'll have some fresh, hot coffee ready when he's done."

"Sure thing, Ma," Johnny said as he stepped out the back door and into the fresh white snow.

Ma turned to the other children, who were still finishing up their pancakes. "What are the rest of you going to do this afternoon?"

"I'm going to go sledding down the big hill," said Kimmy.

"Me too," said Jimmy. Jaimie nodded in agreement. The remaining boys just shrugged.

When all the children were finally finished and the dishes done, each went their own direction. Kimmy was busy finding gloves, boots, and coats for herself and the two boys. Jimmy and Jaimie went to the basement to find three sleds. Justin went to his room to organize his rock collection, and Jason was busy in the living room building a city out of Legos. Only Jared seemed unsure of what to do. At first he thought he would reread his *Flying Squirrel* mystery, but then he remembered he had lent it to his friend Nathan Gruff.

After wandering around for a while, Jared decided to go outside. He was so bundled up in a bright blue parka, boots, snow pants, gloves, a hat, and a scarf that he looked like a big blue marshmallow. First he went to the barn to see how Pa and Johnny were coming along with the firewood. They didn't seem to need any help, so he went to watch the others sled. On the way he saw some large icicles hanging from the roof of the garden shed.

He pulled down an exceptionally large one and began to lick it like a popsicle. It was so large and so cold that it wasn't long before he became tired of it and tried to throw it on the ground. But of course, the now wet icicle was stuck to his glove.

"Come off of there, you stupid icicle," said Jared irritatedly.

The icicle, however, refused to obey his command. The harder he tried to rid himself of that darn icicle, the harder it seemed to stick to his glove. Finally, with a mighty heave of his hand, the icicle came loose and flew through the air. It flew through the air and right through the kitchen window as Jared stood and watched helplessly.

Jared stared at the broken window. The broken window seemed to stare back. Jared didn't know what to do. How was he going to explain the broken window to his ma and pa?

He decided he had better go in and see what Ma Curlytail had to say. As he entered the house through the back door, he heard his mother humming as she dusted in the living room. The happy sound of her humming made Jared feel even guiltier and more scared then he had felt outside.

"I need time to think," he mumbled under his breath. He slowly began to take off all of his outdoor garments. When he was finished he took his things to the laundry room to dry. As he came back into the kitchen, he saw his mother looking at the broken window.

"What in the world happened here?" she was saying to herself.

Jared cleared his throat to speak, but nothing came out.

She turned and looked to see who had entered the kitchen. "Hello, sweetie. Do you know what happened?" Jared didn't reply. "Well, we can't have all this cold air coming in. Would you please go get your father so he can board up this window?"

"Sure, Ma." Jared turned to go get his boots and coat back on.

The trip to the barn seemed like an eternity instead of the few minutes it actually took. The whole way there, Jared kept thinking, *Why didn't I tell Ma?* He had never kept the truth from anyone before, and he was really beginning to regret doing so now.

He told Pa what Ma wanted. Pa began to search for the supplies he would need to temporarily board up the window. "I think there is a scrap of plywood around here somewhere."

Once Pa found the plywood, Jared helped him carry in the tools and supplies he needed. He tried to tell Ma and Pa what had happened, but the words just wouldn't come out. By this time all the other children had returned to the house and were busy chattering to each other and taking off their cold, wet clothes. With so many other children chattering, Jared's silence went unnoticed.

"Well, that should take care of the problem until I can get to Mr. Flock's to get a new pane of glass," Pa said.

"What happened to the window?" Kimmy asked.

"I don't know," said Ma. "When I came into the kitchen it was just broken. I don't suppose any of you children know what happened?"

A chorus of no was heard 'round the kitchen.

"Well, everyone out of the kitchen now; I need to clean up this glass before I make dinner."

Soon dinner was ready—warm, fresh biscuits, greens, and homemade macaroni and cheese. Everyone found their seat and bowed their heads. Pa asked the blessing, and Ma began to pass the food around. Dinner, which was usually a fun and lively affair, went on as usual, but Jared could hardly eat.

"What's the matter, Jared?" Ma asked. "You haven't even touched your macaroni and cheese, and I know it's your favorite."

"I guess I'm just not very hungry."

She got up and felt his forehead. "Aren't you feeling well?"

"I'm fine," he replied, and then he burst into tears.

Everyone stopped what they were doing and looked questioningly at him. Ma gently hugged him and waited until he was ready to say what was on his mind. It was several minutes before he could stop crying. Then he wiped his eyes and looked at his parents.

He began to explain in a sniffly but brave voice. "I broke the window by accident. I was licking a huge icicle and it stuck to my glove, and when I tried to get it off, it went flying through the window."

Jimmy started to chuckle but quickly stopped when Pa gave him the "or else" look. The others thought it best to sit quietly.

"I tried to tell you when you came into the kitchen," Jared continued. "But I got scared, and nothing would come out. I'm so sorry, Ma. Are you going to punish me for not telling you right away?"

Ma kissed Jared on the forehead and smiled her sweet smile. "I don't think so. I think your conscience has punished you enough."

"Yeah, I felt so bad the whole time."

"And maybe next time you will remember your ma and I never get upset at accidents if you kids tell the truth," said Pa.

Jared began to eat his macaroni. "Thanks, Pa."

Ma started to walk back to her seat. "Well, it's good to see your appetite has returned."

Jared smiled and shoved another bite in his mouth. Telling the truth had given him a huge appetite. But even more than that, telling the truth made him feel good inside!